What is Faith's secret?

MISS ABIGAIL LOOKED from Faith to Mandie to Joe. "Do y'all think we would have time for a cup of tea, Amanda?" she asked.

"I'm sorry, Miss Abigail, but I'm afraid my mother will be wondering where I am," Mandie replied, wishing with all her might that she could stay.

"And I have to do some chores for my mother, and I promised Mrs. Shaw I would walk home with Mandie," Joe put in as he started down the steps.

"We'll have tea next time you come back, then," Miss Abigail said.

"Yes, ma'am," Mandie agreed. She turned to follow Joe, who was walking on toward the lane. "Goodbye."

Suddenly Faith hurried to catch up with Mandie. "Please come back tomorrow after school. Please," she whispered to Mandie.

Why was Faith acting so mysterious? Mandie looked back at the house and saw that Miss Abigail was standing on the porch, watching them.

"Is something wrong?" Mandie whispered.

"I don't know," Faith whispered back. "I have a problem. Please come."

Don't miss any of Mandie Shaw's
page-turning mysteries!

And look for the next book, coming soon!

The Mystery at Miss Abigail's

Lois Gladys Leppard

BANTAM BOOKS
NEW YORK · TORONTO · LONDON · SYDNEY · AUCKLAND

RL 2.6, ages 7–10
THE MYSTERY AT MISS ABIGAIL'S
A Bantam Skylark Book / November 1999

*With thanks to
Beverly Horowitz,
who caused it all*

1

A Whispered Plea

"I HOPE YOU CAN come visit often," Miss Abigail said to Mandie. "I know Faith will be lonely without her grandmother." She and Mandie were standing on Miss Abigail's wide veranda, watching as Faith Winters told her grandmother goodbye. Mrs. Chapman stepped into the buggy with Dr. Woodard for their journey to the train station.

"Oh, yes, ma'am, Miss Abigail. Thank you," Mandie replied, her blue eyes shining. "I'll be over every time my mother will allow me to come."

Miss Abigail lived in the finest house in Swain County, North Carolina. She had had the building materials brought, piece by piece, on wagons over the rough road across the Nantahala Mountains ten years earlier.

After her white, two-story house had been finished, Miss Abigail had filled it with a lifetime of treasures. Unlike the other settlers, Miss Abigail never revealed where she had come from or why she had chosen to live in such an isolated territory. Nevertheless, the other women in the Charley Gap community had soon accepted her as a friend. Although Miss Abigail was very wealthy, she was not uppity and was eager to mingle with the others.

Nine-year-old Amanda Shaw, who was called Mandie by her friends, loved visiting the lady and looking at the rich furnishings, the likes of which she had never seen before. She had been delighted when Miss Abigail said she would take in her friend Faith while Faith's grandmother went to New York for medical treatment. Now Mandie could visit Faith every chance she got and enjoy being in Miss Abigail's house.

Mandie's good friend Joe Woodard, the doctor's son, had been talking to his father. When Dr. Woodard shook the reins to drive up the lane, Joe walked back to the porch to join Mandie. Faith stood in the yard waving until the buggy carrying her grandmother was out of sight. Then she slowly came up the steps.

"Faith, I have to go home now. I promised my mother I would as soon as your grandmother left. I'll see you at school tomorrow," Mandie told the tall, dark-haired girl, who was trying hard not to cry. Mandie knew this was the first time Faith had been separated from her grandmother.

Miss Abigail looked from Faith to Mandie to Joe. "Do y'all think we would have time for a cup of tea, Amanda?" she asked.

"I'm sorry, Miss Abigail, but I'm afraid my mother will be wondering where I am," Mandie replied, wishing with all her might that she could stay.

"And I have to do some chores for my mother, and I promised Mrs. Shaw I would walk home with Mandie," Joe put in as he started down the steps.

Mandie looked back at Faith, who had not said a word. The girl seemed to be in deep thought about something, probably about how much she was going to miss her grandmother.

"We'll have tea next time you come back, then," Miss Abigail said.

"Yes, ma'am," Mandie agreed. She turned to follow Joe, who was walking on toward the lane. "Goodbye."

Suddenly Faith hurried to catch up with Mandie. "Please come back tomorrow after school. Please," she whispered to Mandie.

Mandie looked at her friend in surprise. "All right, if my mother says I can," she told Faith. She noticed that Joe was going ahead to the road.

"Please try real hard to come," Faith said, still whispering.

Why was Faith acting so mysterious? Mandie looked back at the house and saw that Miss Abigail was standing on the porch, watching them.

"Is something wrong?" Mandie whispered.

"I don't know," Faith whispered back. "I have a problem. Please come."

"Come on, Mandie!" Joe called. "I've got to get home."

"All right," Mandie replied. "I have to go now, Faith. I'll talk to you at recess tomorrow." She smiled at Faith and hurried to catch up with

Joe, and then turned to wave. Faith was walking slowly toward the porch.

"Come on, Mandie. Get a move on," Joe told her as he started on down the road.

Mandie rushed to keep up with him. "There's something wrong. Faith wanted me to promise that I would absolutely come over to Miss Abigail's after school tomorrow. She said she has a problem. I wonder what it could be?"

"She's already lonely because her grandmother has gone to New York, and she doesn't really know Miss Abigail very well, and now she has to live with her until Mrs. Chapman comes back," Joe said.

"Do you think that's all it's about?" Mandie asked thoughtfully.

"Probably," Joe replied.

"I don't know." Mandie looked up at the tall boy. "I hope that doctor in New York will be able to help Mrs. Chapman's face." Faith's grandmother had been badly burned in a house fire.

"My father said scars from burns are almost always permanent," Joe replied, looking down at Mandie. "But the doctor he is taking Mrs.

Chapman to see has been studying new procedures, so he may be able to do some good."

"I hope so," Mandie said, kicking a pebble. It would be terrible to be scarred for life. "All the women in the neighborhood will be meeting at Miss Abigail's house tomorrow afternoon to plan what they can do about the needlework Mrs. Chapman does for other people." Mrs. Chapman was a seamstress. "I wanted to go, but they're doing this before school lets out."

"You don't know how to do that kind of sewing, Mandie. You said so yourself," Joe reminded her as they walked along the road.

Mandie took big steps to keep up with Joe's long legs. "But I want to learn," she said. "I'm nine years old, it's high time I did."

"I don't think you'll have much time for it. You told me you wanted to help the men fix up Mrs. Chapman's property while she's gone. You can't do but one thing at a time," Joe said.

Mrs. Chapman and Faith had recently moved into the old Conley place. The house and the land were in bad shape and Mandie's father had organized a group to do repairs.

"Well, I can do a little bit of one and then a

little of the other, that's what I can do," Mandie replied. "I want to learn how to tat and do those fancy embroidery stitches for myself. And the women are planning on making new curtains and dresser scarves and counterpanes and things, and I need to learn how to make those, too."

"What for, Mandie?" Joe asked.

Mandie frowned slightly. "All women need to know about such things. *If* I ever get married when I grow up, I'll be able to make my own."

Joe laughed. "That's a long time in the future," he said.

"Miss Abigail said she would teach the women who don't know how to do all those things," Mandie said. "That means they will probably all meet at Miss Abigail's house whenever they get together." Her eyes widened. "I'd just love to go to Miss Abigail's house."

"You told Miss Abigail you would come and visit Faith while she's staying there," Joe reminded her. They came to the lane leading to Mandie's house and stopped on the road.

"I know, but if I could go to Miss Abigail's for these lessons, it would be like a big party. I'm sure she'll serve cake on her fine china plates and tea in those beautiful cups and saucers that she keeps in the china closet," Mandie said wistfully to Joe.

"What an excuse to go visit someone!" Joe exclaimed. "I'd better get on home now. See you in the morning." He turned to go back up the road and on to his house.

"Goodbye," Mandie called to him. She hurried down the lane to her house. *I wonder if my mother knows what Miss Abigail is planning.*

She ran up the steps and went through the front door. Her parents were in the parlor, sitting by the fire that burned in the huge stone fireplace. Her father was reading and her mother was knitting. Windy, Mandie's kitten, was curled up asleep on the hearth.

"I'm back," Mandie called, removing her coat, tam, and gloves and hanging them on pegs by the doorway that led to the kitchen.

"So I see," Mr. Shaw said, looking up with a teasing smile.

Mandie pulled a stool over near the fireplace and sat down, stretching out her hands to warm them. She smiled up at her father. "When are the men going to start work on Mrs. Chapman's place?"

"Most likely it will be Friday or Saturday," he replied.

"I want to help," Mandie declared.

"There won't be much you can do," Mr. Shaw said. "We'll be repairing boards in the house and in the barn and refencing the chicken yard. A lot of carpenter work needs to be done first."

"I could help with cleaning up in the yard," Mandie said hopefully.

"No, I don't think you'd better plan on participating in any of the work right now. We aren't sure exactly what all we have to do until we examine boards for rot. Maybe later there will be something you can do," Mr. Shaw told her with a smile.

Mandie sighed and turned to her mother. "Mama, what is Miss Abigail planning to do about Mrs. Chapman's needlework orders?" she asked.

Without looking up from her knitting, Mrs. Shaw replied, "All the women are going over to Miss Abigail's right after the noon meal tomorrow, and we'll decide then how to handle the matter."

"Mama, I want to learn all that needlework. Faith knows how because she helps her grandmother. Please ask Miss Abigail to let me help—please," Mandie begged, leaning toward her mother from the stool where she was sitting.

Mrs. Shaw paused as she looped the yarn around the needle to make a stitch. "I'm not sure you can help, Amanda," she replied. "From what I understand, we'll be working on the needlework right after noontime every day or two, or whatever time we agree to spend on it. That way we can all get back home and get our suppers on the table on time. You don't get out of school until late afternoon."

"If I came straight to Miss Abigail's from school, I could get there before y'all leave, couldn't I?" Mandie eagerly asked.

"I just don't know, Amanda. I'll have to wait and see what the women decide to do," Mrs. Shaw replied. She continued with her knitting.

"And they will decide tomorrow, won't they?" Mandie asked.

"Yes," Mrs. Shaw said. "Have you seen your sister this afternoon?"

"Irene? No, I haven't, Mama. Where is she supposed to be?" Mandie asked.

"She said she was going over to Mrs. Chapman's place to catch up with you and Joe," Mrs. Shaw said.

"But, Mama, we didn't go to Mrs. Chapman's house. Mrs. Chapman and Faith went over to Miss Abigail's to wait for Dr. Woodard there," Mandie explained. "Remember when Joe came by to walk with me, he said everyone would be at Miss Abigail's?"

Mrs. Shaw frowned as she looked up from her knitting. "I suppose everyone was in a hurry because Dr. Woodard was having to make that last-minute call. I reckon I didn't really pay much attention to what was being said."

Mr. Shaw put down his book. "I imagine Irene will be back soon. When she didn't find anyone at Mrs. Chapman's, she probably went on to Miss Abigail's and was too late to catch up with you and Joe, Amanda."

Mandie wondered if her sister had slipped off to meet Tommy Lester. Irene was forever disappearing, and lots of times, Mandie knew, she met Tommy somewhere. Their mother didn't approve of the boy's always hanging around, interfering with Mandie and Irene's chores.

"It was kindhearted of Miss Abigail to ask Faith to live with her while her grandmother is in New York," Mrs. Shaw said thoughtfully. "I hope and pray the doctors up there can do something about the scars on her face."

"Yes, ma'am, so do I, and I also hope Faith will enjoy living with Miss Abigail," Mandie said as Windy rose, stretched, and jumped into her lap. Mandie rubbed Windy's head, and Windy curled up and started purring. Then Mandie remembered Faith's parting words. "Mama, is it all right if I go to Miss Abigail's right after school tomorrow? Faith asked me to please be sure and come over. She was whispering and looked worried about something. I asked her what was wrong and she said she didn't know."

"Amanda, you will be seeing Faith at school tomorrow," her mother reminded her.

"I know, but we don't have any privacy at school, and the only time we have to talk is at recess, and that's too short to do anything but eat."

"Faith is probably still shy around Miss Abigail. After all, Faith and her grandmother haven't been living in Charley Gap long enough to really know anyone. Naturally Faith turns to you for friendship because she has become acquainted with you at school. Don't make a mountain out of a molehill, Amanda."

"May I at least walk to Miss Abigail's with Faith after school tomorrow? Joe will probably go with us if I ask him, if you're worried about me walking home from there by myself, and besides, you and the other women may still be there." Mandie said all this in a big rush. "Please, Mama."

Mrs. Shaw sighed loudly as she counted stitches. "All right, Amanda, but you are not to stay too long at Miss Abigail's. And yes, you should ask Joe to go with you. Now, I want to finish this section before I have to put supper on the table. You go look around outside and see if you can find Irene, but mind you don't go off anywhere."

Mandie smiled as she put down her kitten and stood up. "Thank you, Mama," she said, going to get her coat and tam from the pegs. Glancing back at her mother, she said, "I'm so proud of this tam you knitted for me. I hated wearing bonnets."

Mrs. Shaw looked up to smile at her. "I figured you were getting a little too old for bonnets."

Mr. Shaw laid his book on the table next to his chair and rose. "I'll go out to the barn and check on everything for the night," he told Mrs Shaw as he too took his coat and hat down from the pegs. Turning to smile down at Mandie, he added, "Then Amanda and I could probably get supper started while you finish your knitting."

"Thank you, Jim, that would be a great help," Mrs. Shaw said.

Mandie and her father walked to the door. "Maybe we can find Irene and she can help too," Mandie said as they went into the yard. Windy followed them. "You know, Daddy, I'm a little worried about Faith," Mandie added. "I believe she does have a problem of some kind, the way she was acting."

"In that case you're going to have to help her solve the problem. I know how much you like mysteries," Mr. Shaw replied with a big grin.

"I just hope it's something I can help her with," Mandie replied seriously. She glanced up the driveway. "Oh, here comes Irene now." She pointed.

"Well, at least we don't have to look for her," Mr. Shaw said as they walked on to the barn.

"I wonder where she's been," Mandie said thoughtfully. Her sister seemed to come and go whenever she pleased without too much trouble from their parents. Mandie sighed. She was sure that if she did such things, she would end up in all kinds of trouble. "But she's two years older than I am," she added under her breath.

I just hope Irene doesn't want to walk with Faith and Joe and me to Miss Abigail's tomorrow, Mandie thought. If Faith had a secret to tell her, she might not want to talk with Irene around.

2
No Luck!

THE NEXT MORNING Mandie rushed to the main road, where Joe was waiting for her to walk to school. Irene followed.

"I have permission to walk home with Faith if you'll go with us, Joe," Mandie told him as he took her books. He always carried them to and from school for her.

Before Joe could say anything, Irene asked, "What are you walking home with Faith for?"

Mandie quickly looked at her as the three walked down the road. "There's something we want to talk about," she said.

"Well, count me out," Irene said. "I'm not going by Miss Abigail's. I don't think that Faith is friendly, anyway. She stares at everyone and never says a word."

"Oh, Irene, you know the reason for that," Mandie protested. "If your house had burned down and your parents were killed and the only person you had left was your grandmother, you wouldn't be friendly either."

"I know that's a terrible thing that happened, but she could at least speak now and then," Irene insisted. "Anyhow, I'm not going with y'all to Miss Abigail's, I'm going straight home after school."

"Mama will probably still be at Miss Abigail's," Mandie reminded her. "The women are meeting there today to make plans for the needlework they're going to do for Mrs. Chapman."

"Well, I know I'm not about to go by there, then. You won't catch me doing all that needlework," Irene replied, swinging her book bag.

"Is that why you're going by Miss Abigail's after school?" Joe asked Mandie.

"Not exactly," Mandie told him. Irene didn't seem to be listening but was gazing down the road. "Faith and I have something we want to talk about, and we won't be able to do it at school."

"Well now, that sounds mysterious," Joe said with a big grin, looking down at Mandie. He gave her braid a playful tug.

Mandie looked up at his teasing brown eyes. "Oh, it is mysterious," she said, returning his grin.

Irene looked at her sister and said, "One of your silly mysteries."

"What's the mystery all about?" Joe asked.

"I don't know yet. That's why I have to talk to Faith. Then I'll let you know," Mandie promised.

When the three arrived at the schoolhouse, Faith was already in her seat. Mandie passed by to whisper to her, "I have permission to walk home with you after school."

Faith pushed back her long dark hair and smiled up at Mandie. "I'm glad," she said.

Mandie wished the day away; the morning lessons seemed to last forever. At recess, Faith joined her and Joe to eat lunch.

"Joe is going to walk with us after school so he can go on home with me," Mandie said to Faith. "My mother told me to ask him."

"Oh," Faith said, glancing at Joe, who was sitting on a fallen tree trunk across from where she and Mandie sat on tree stumps.

"Oh, don't worry," Joe told Faith. He raked his fingers through his already messy hair. "I'm only coming along for the walk. You and Mandie can keep your secrets. When I get involved in a mystery with Mandie, it gets to be complicated sometimes." He bit into his biscuit.

"But we don't have a mystery. I only want to talk to Mandie about something," Faith said, taking a biscuit with ham in it out of her lunch basket.

"I consider that a mystery," Joe teased. "You girls can talk all you want. I'll just wait for Mandie when we get to Miss Abigail's house."

Mandie was more curious than ever now. She looked around the schoolyard. Out of the corner of her eye, she noticed her sister sitting with Tommy Lester in a clearing away from the other students. Irene was probably asking him to walk home with her, since she knew that Mandie and Joe would not be going straight home.

The bell rang and everyone jumped up and closed their lunch pails and baskets. Mandie,

Joe, and Faith joined the rush into the school-house, where everyone settled down for their afternoon lessons.

When the bell rang again later for dismissal, Mandie was the first one to the coatrack to get her things. There was no time to waste—she was on her way to discovering a new mystery!

When the three arrived at Miss Abigail's house, Mandie gazed around the yard. There was no sign of a horse or wagon. That meant her mother and the other women weren't there. Then she noticed Miss Abigail sitting alone at the far end of the front porch.

"Come in," Miss Abigail said, motioning toward the steps. "I'm glad y'all could come home with Faith. I'll just go make that pot of tea I promised last time. Come on inside." She opened the front door. "It's a little too cool out here."

Miss Abigail led the way into the front hall-way. Mandie, Joe, and Faith followed, removed their wraps, and hung them on the coat tree.

"I'll go ask Miss Dicey to get things ready,"

Miss Abigail told them. Pointing to her left, she said, "Y'all just go in there in the parlor and make yourselves comfortable. I'll be right back."

The three young people entered the parlor and sat down on a velvet settee. Mandie leaned over and whispered to Faith, "Who is Miss Dicey?"

"Miss Abigail hired her to help with the housework," Faith explained. Then she smiled. "I suppose having me here will make extra work."

Miss Abigail had returned and heard the remark as she stepped into the room. "Oh, no, dear, that's not the reason at all," she explained, sitting beside the fireplace. "You see, if I'm going to have all these women coming here for the needlework, I thought I needed a little help. As far as you are concerned, it's a privilege to have you. You're no trouble at all."

Faith blushed. "Thank you, Miss Abigail. It's a privilege to stay here while my grandmother is gone."

Mandie wondered when she and Faith could have a private talk. It would have to wait, for now Miss Dicey came into the room to prepare a table near the settee for tea. She was probably the tallest, thinnest woman Mandie had ever seen. Her brown hair had a few strands of gray in it, but her face was young-looking and pleasant as she caught Mandie's eye and smiled at her. Mandie smiled back as she watched Miss Dicey spread a cloth on the table and then leave the room.

Turning to Miss Abigail, Mandie asked, "Have all the women already been here and gone?"

"Yes, they didn't stay long today. We only made our plans, and that didn't take much time," Miss Abigail replied. "They'll all be back on Wednesday to begin lessons and start work."

"But how can they start working if they have to take lessons?" Mandie asked, puzzled by Miss Abigail's remark.

"Those who know how to do some kinds of needlework will begin working on things they know how to do. I'll try to teach the other women," Miss Abigail explained. "We'll have a large group who can turn out lots of needlework for Mrs. Chapman's orders." She glanced at Faith. "We'll be able to do a lot more than you and your grandmother have. I hope to get new customers and also get more orders from the ones your grandmother already has."

"I'm sure you will, Miss Abigail," Faith replied. "My grandmother has had to turn down so many orders because the two of us couldn't do all that work. We will be grateful for your help in seeing that the needlework can continue while she's gone." She paused a moment. "I just hope she doesn't have to stay in New York long."

Mandie spoke up. "But, Faith, she has to stay long enough to see if the doctor there can do anything to help her."

"That's right," Joe added. "My father said it might take months."

"Months?" Faith repeated.

"Don't worry, dear," Miss Abigail said. "I know you want your grandmother to stay in New York as long as is necessary. Just think how it will be if she can come back home in better shape than she was when she went! Why, Mrs. Chapman may even decide to teach again once her face is repaired. Then she wouldn't have to do all this needlework."

"I'm sorry to sound selfish, Miss Abigail,"

Faith said. "She's all I have left, and I'll be wishing the time away until she can come home."

"We'll help you wish it away," Mandie said with a big smile. "I'm so glad to have a friend near enough to visit."

Just then Miss Dicey returned with the tea on a large tray and set it on the table. She straightened up and looked at Miss Abigail.

"Everything looks fine, Miss Dicey, thank you," Miss Abigail told her. Miss Dicey smiled and left the room. Miss Abigail began pouring the tea. "Y'all come on now and help yourselves to the cookies," she told the young people.

As soon as everyone was served and seated again, Mandie asked, "Miss Abigail, I would like to learn all that needlework you are planning to teach. Will you be doing it after I get out of school?"

"Oh, dear, that is a problem," Miss Abigail said, setting her cup on the table. "You see, some of the women can only come in the mornings, and the others will be here in the afternoon. I'm not sure yet how long those afternoon sessions will last. Some of the women have to be home to care for their children, and others have to get supper ready."

"That sounds like you'll be tied up all day long," Joe remarked.

"No, not really. We won't be working every day. We'll begin this Wednesday, and our next day together will be Friday," Miss Abigail explained. "On Friday and Saturday the men will be working on Mrs. Chapman's property. They will be taking plenty of food with them and working as late as the light holds."

"So the women are planning to do their work at the same time the men do theirs?" Mandie asked.

"That's right," Miss Abigail said. "It'll be more convenient that way for everyone."

"I'll have to decide whether to come here for the needlework or go with my father to help the men," Mandie said thoughtfully. "My father said there would be nothing I could do at the beginning, but later I would like to help them."

Joe grinned. "You come here for the needlework. I'll go help my father and the other men, and I'll let you know what goes on."

Mandie tightened her lips and frowned at him. "Somebody has to tend to the food whenever they get ready to eat," she said. "I could do that."

"Yes, and speaking of tending to food, I think we'd better start home," Joe replied. "My mother didn't know I was coming by here, and I have things to do at home before suppertime." He stood up.

Mandie realized it was time to go, but Miss Abigail had stayed with them every minute, and she and Faith had not had time to talk. Disappointed, she rose. "I'll see you tomorrow at school, Faith. Maybe I can come by again after we get out."

"Please do," Faith said with a sad little smile. She also rose.

Miss Abigail stood up. "It was nice having you young people come visit. Please do come back tomorrow, or anytime you like."

"Thank you for the tea," Mandie said.

"And I thank you, Miss Abigail. The cookies were delicious," Joe told her.

Miss Abigail walked with them to get their wraps in the huge front hall. As they passed a large china cabinet, Mandie paused to look through the glass doors at the beautiful china and glassware on the shelves inside.

"Miss Abigail, you have such pretty dishes!" she exclaimed.

"Yes, it has taken me many years to collect all those things. Each and every one is a treasure," Miss Abigail said.

"I've never seen so much in one place before," Mandie said, still admiring the cabinet's contents.

"Someday you'll have the same thing," Miss Abigail assured her. "When you are old enough to be on your own, you will collect things too."

"My mother keeps her china in cabinets with wooden doors, and you can't see it unless they're open," Joe remarked. "I think she ought to get a cabinet like that one, where you can see inside."

Mandie turned to look at Faith, who was standing back across the hallway. "Faith, you're so lucky to live here," Mandie said with a smile.

Faith dropped her eyes. "I know," she said softly.

When they stepped outside onto the porch, Mandie hoped that Miss Abigail would go back inside so that she could speak privately to Faith, but Miss Abigail stayed right there with them. Faith seemed to be nervous as she glanced at Mandie and then at Miss Abigail. *There's really something wrong,* Mandie decided.

Joe walked ahead up the lane to the road. "Come on, Mandie. Let's go," he called back. He stopped to look at her.

Mandie squeezed Faith's hand. "I'll see you at school tomorrow, and then maybe I can walk home with you again."

Faith nodded.

Mandie hurried to catch up with Joe. As they reached the main road, she said, "I didn't get a chance to speak to Faith. Do you think Miss Abigail will stay right with us every time we visit?"

"Mandie, I don't know. I think Miss Abigail was just being nice. I don't believe she wanted to interfere," Joe replied.

"I know that, but my mother doesn't stay with me and my friends when they come to visit," Mandie protested.

"Neither does my mother, but that's just the

way Miss Abigail was raised," Joe replied. "She's different."

"I'll ask my mother if I can visit Faith on Wednesday," Mandie said. "Maybe then Miss Abigail will be involved with teaching needlework, and Faith and I can have a few minutes to talk."

Joe looked down at her and smiled. "I imagine Miss Abigail is going to have her hands full."

"I'm going to ask my father if I can come with the men who are going to work on Faith's house on Saturday. I can serve the food," Mandie told him as they continued down the road.

"Mandie, you just want to get involved in everything, and there's not enough time in the day for you to go to school and do all these extra things," Joe told her. "And you do have to do homework sometime or other, remember."

"I know," Mandie said, stomping her feet in her high-top button-up shoes as she walked. "I'll figure it all out somehow. I'll just be glad when school gets out so I'll have more time."

"It's a long time till summer holidays," Joe reminded her.

"The most important thing right now is to get a chance to talk to Faith and find out what's worrying her," Mandie said with a big sigh. "I know there's something very wrong."

"Now, how do you know that, Mandie?" Joe said with a teasing smile.

Mandie put her arms around herself and squeezed. "I can just feel it in my bones." She grinned up at him.

3

Making Plans

"MAMA, DO YOU THINK you'll still be at Miss Abigail's house Wednesday when I get out of school?" Mandie asked as she laid her fork down on her plate. The Shaws were in the middle of supper.

"I have no idea, Amanda," Mrs. Shaw replied, taking a sip of her coffee. "Even Miss Abigail doesn't know our schedule. She said we could just work that out after we get together on Wednesday."

"Would it be all right if I came by Miss Abigail's house from school just in case you are still there?" Mandie asked, holding her breath for the reply.

"I don't know what good that would do you," Mrs. Shaw said. "We'd be almost ready to go home by then, so you wouldn't have any opportunity to learn anything. Besides, I don't think you can get involved in this needlework. You have homework to do, and you certainly can't let anything interfere with that."

"Miss Abigail said y'all would probably meet on Friday, too," Mandie told her. "If I came over Friday, maybe y'all would still be there and I could learn a little and I would have all weekend to get my homework done. Besides, Mr. Tallant very seldom gives us homework for the weekend. Please, Mama, please!"

Mrs. Shaw took a deep breath. "Well, I suppose you could on Friday, but just remember, we may be gone by the time you get out of school."

Mandie gave her mother a big smile. "Thank you, Mama. I'll come by Miss Abigail's on Friday, then."

"I don't understand why you want to learn all that needlework. That's hard work," Irene said from across the table.

"I want to because I want to. That's why," Mandie said, frowning at her.

"Just remember this," Mrs. Shaw told Mandie. "If I'm not there, you are to come straight home and not linger to visit with Faith. Do you understand?"

"Yes, ma'am," Mandie replied.

"Remember, Etta, all of us men will be working until dark on Friday at Mrs. Chapman's place," Mr. Shaw said. "We're taking our supper with us, so you won't have to rush home because of that. We'll be working there Saturday, too."

"I know, Jim," Mrs. Shaw replied.

"Oh, Daddy," Mandie began, her bright blue eyes crinkling, "do you think I could go with you Saturday and help with the food for the men? If I could, that would save y'all a lot of time. Please."

Mr. Shaw's own blue eyes crinkled as he smiled at his daughter. "Amanda, I do believe you are trying to get involved in everything that's going on, and you know as well as I do that that's impossible."

Mandie pretended to be hurt because her father didn't want her to work with him. She pouted as she said, "I only want to help because you're helping, Daddy. It wouldn't hurt anything to let me go with you, would it?"

"Amanda, sometimes I just don't know what to do with you," Mr. Shaw replied with a grin. Turning to his wife, he asked, "Do you especially need Amanda here Saturday?"

"I suppose Irene can do whatever needs to be done," Mrs. Shaw said.

"I'm not going to do all the work while Mandie runs off somewhere!" Irene quickly said.

"Most of the time I do all the work while you run off somewhere," Mandie came back at her. "Besides, I wouldn't be exactly running off. I'd be going to help with Mrs. Chapman's house."

"Here now, girls," Mrs. Shaw told the two. "I won't have any of that. Irene, you will stay here and help me with the work Saturday, unless you're willing to help your father at Mrs. Chapman's place."

"No, thank you," Irene replied with a big frown, tossing her long dark hair behind her shoulders. "I'll stay here and work."

"Then we've got everything settled," Mrs. Shaw said, finishing her food. "Girls, eat up. We need to get the table cleared off so I can use it to lay out a pattern for a dress."

"A pattern for a dress?" Mandie repeated

excitedly. "Are you going to make me or Irene a new dress?"

"Not this time," Mrs. Shaw replied. "It's for Faith. Since her clothes were destroyed when their house burned down, she has only two dresses. Miss Abigail has donated several of her own dresses to be cut up and made into clothes for Faith. I volunteered to make one, Mrs. Woodard will do one, and Miss Dicey will make the other one. And while I think about it, neither of you is to breathe a word of this to Faith. Miss Abigail wanted to keep it secret and will give the dresses to Faith herself when we get them made. Just remember that."

"Oh, how nice of Miss Abigail!" Mandie exclaimed. "The girls at school talk about Faith and wonder why she wears the same dress almost all the time. It would be wonderful for her to have something new."

"But how will Miss Abigail's fine clothes look on Faith?" Irene asked. "The dresses might be too good to wear to school, and then the other girls would laugh at Faith."

"There won't be any problem with these dresses," Mrs. Shaw said. "Irene, since Faith is about your size, I'll need to have you try them on for hems and such."

"Long as I don't have to wear them," Irene remarked in a low voice.

Mandie sat there trying to figure out how she could get a chance to talk with Faith alone. If she could just walk with Faith to Miss Abigail's house after school, they could talk. Joe could come too—Mandie knew he would not eavesdrop, even if they stopped to talk.

"Mama, will it be all right if I just walk by Miss Abigail's house with Faith after school now and then? You know Miss Abigail lives near the school, and it will only take five minutes longer to do that," Mandie told her mother. "Joe will walk with us. And Joe and I won't stop to talk there. We can just come straight on home."

"Amanda, I know how much you appreciate having Faith for a friend, since no other girls your age live near here, but I do think we should slow down with all this visiting at Miss Abigail's house," Mrs. Shaw said, finishing the contents of her coffee cup and replacing it in the saucer.

"But that wouldn't really be a visit, Mama," Mandie protested. "It would just be making a little circle a little bit out of the way. Faith doesn't have any friends because she and her grandmother are new here. And we won't stop at Miss Abigail's. We'll just keep walking on home, and we can walk extra fast to make up for it. Please, Mama."

Mrs. Shaw looked at Mr. Shaw. "She's certainly your daughter, Jim. I give up. You take over."

Mr. Shaw smiled at his wife. "All right, you and Joe can circle by Miss Abigail's house with Faith after school now and then, but just remember, this doesn't include stopping," he said. "You are to walk straight on home from there, and we'll be keeping an eye on the time you get home from school. Understand?"

"Thank you, Daddy," Mandie said, beaming. "We'll walk extra fast."

"Well, don't count me in on this extra walking," Irene told her sister. "I'll be coming straight home from school every day."

Mandie breathed a sigh of relief. "That's all right, Irene. You don't have to walk out of the way with us."

Mrs. Shaw rose. "Now let's get this table cleared off in a hurry."

Mandie could hardly wait to tell Faith she could walk around by Miss Abigail's with her. Maybe Faith would finally discuss whatever was worrying her . . . and maybe Mandie could help.

The next morning Mandie explained to Joe when she met him at the road, "So I have permission to walk with Faith to Miss Abigail's after school, provided I just keep going and don't stop there."

"Mandie, this is kind of crazy," Joe protested as they walked to school. "Faith may not want us tagging along with her all the way to Miss Abigail's house."

"We'll only do it until I get a chance to talk to Faith and find out what her problem is," Mandie explained, hurrying to keep up with Joe.

"She may not have that big of a problem," Joe reminded her. "Remember, she said she just wanted to talk. She's so shy around Miss Abigail— I suppose she would be glad to talk to someone her own age now and then."

"Joe, we don't have to do this every day, just until Faith begins to talk about whatever is troubling her," Mandie said.

"All right, as long as it doesn't cause me to be late getting home," Joe finally agreed.

"Thank you, Joe," Mandie replied as they came to the lane leading to the schoolhouse. She glimpsed Faith going through the front door and began racing toward her. "There's Faith now," she called back to Joe.

By the time Mandie got inside and hung up her coat and tam, Faith had already taken her seat. Mandie hurried down the aisle and leaned over to whisper, "Faith, I have permission to walk around by Miss Abigail's with you after school."

Faith looked up from where she sat next to Esther Rogan. "That's nice," she said, smiling.

Esther tapped Faith on the shoulder. "I want to walk home with you today, Faith. My mother said I could ask Miss Abigail if I could join the needlework classes."

Mandie and Faith both looked at Esther in surprise. Esther had barely spoken to Faith since Faith had started school with them.

"That's nice of you, Esther," Faith told her with a slight smile.

"Is your mother coming too?" Mandie asked.

"No, Mandie," Esther replied. "She can't do that kind of work because of arthritis in her hands. But she said I could, so wait for me at the front door when school is out, Faith."

"I'll be praying that your mother's hands get better, Esther," Mandie told the girl.

Esther gave Mandie a frowning glance. Just then Mr. Tallant walked to the head of the classroom and called the pupils to order. Mandie rushed to her seat.

All day Mandie found herself wondering why Esther wanted to help out with the needlework when she had been so aloof with Faith. *And if she joins us, I'll never get to talk to Faith alone!* Mandie thought, frustrated. Everything seemed to be keeping her from finding out what Faith wanted to talk about.

When the noon recess came, Mandie told Joe about Esther.

"But how can she join in the needlework lessons if the women are having them while we're still in school?" Joe asked as they sat down on a fallen tree trunk.

Mandie realized that Joe was right. Her

mother had said they would probably be finished by the time school was out. Didn't Esther know that?

Faith arrived and sat down with her lunch basket. "This feels so heavy! Miss Dicey must have put an awful lot of food in it," she remarked as she lifted the lid and looked inside. "My goodness, she did!" She opened a white linen napkin wrapped around several pieces of fried chicken.

Mandie and Joe watched as they began eating their biscuits. Today Mandie had ham in hers, and Joe had sausage.

"She's trying to fatten you up," Joe joked.

"I agree," Faith said, and holding out her basket toward Mandie and Joe, she said, "Here, take some of this. I can't eat it all."

Joe reached over and rescued a drumstick. "Thank you!"

Mandie peeked at the contents of the basket. "I don't know, Faith, I'm not used to eating so much at noon."

"Come on, take at least one piece. That will leave me two," Faith insisted as she held up the napkin laden with chicken. "Oh, look, there are three pieces of chocolate cake in the bottom. Now I know she meant this for all of us—three pieces. Mandie, take some chicken."

"Well, all right," Mandie finally agreed as she reached for a drumstick. "Thank you."

"Chocolate cake!" Joe said with a big grin. "I won't refuse that."

"Does she expect you to eat all this and come home and eat supper?" Mandie asked.

"I don't think so," Faith replied with a smile, and bit into a piece of chicken. "She heard me say I eat lunch with y'all."

"Then she must think we don't have enough to eat," Joe said with a laugh.

"She's so nice," Faith said. "She doesn't have any children. I don't believe she's ever been married, so she probably doesn't know how much to give me for lunch."

"Then maybe if you tell her we thank her for the extra lunch she gave you, she'll understand that it was too much," Mandie said.

When the recess was over and everyone was returning to the schoolhouse, Esther caught up with Faith. "Don't forget to wait for me when school lets out."

"All right," Faith said as Esther rushed past them into the building.

Mandie looked at Faith with a frown. "My mother said the women will probably be doing the needlework while we're in school and will be finished by the time we get out, so how can Esther participate in the classes?" Mandie asked.

Faith frowned and said, "You're right. I heard Miss Abigail say they would probably do all the work while I'm in school, but I suppose if Esther wants to walk home with me and ask Miss Abigail, she can."

"Yes, if we tried to explain everything to her, she'd probably think we were just trying to get rid of her," Mandie agreed.

As they reached the front door of the schoolhouse, Joe turned to look at the girls. "I'll sure be glad when all this scheduling gets fixed and things settle down to normal again."

"With all this work going on, it's going to take a long time for things to settle down," Mandie told him as they stepped inside the building.

As she spoke, Mandie realized that Faith looked sad. "But just think of all the fun this is going to be," Mandie said with a laugh. "It's going to liven up Charley Gap. Nothing ever happens around here. I'm sure glad you came along, Faith." She took off her coat and tam to hang on the pegs by the door.

"I'm glad we did too, Mandie," Faith said, removing her coat and hat and hanging them up.

"Me too, Faith," Joe said as he hung up his jacket. "And I can't wait to work with the men on your house."

"You are growing up, Joe Woodard," Mandie said teasingly as she took her seat.

During the afternoon, Mandie thought about Esther. *I won't say a thing about the sewing schedule to her. Let Miss Abigail tell her.* Mandie didn't want Esther thinking she was not wanted . . . but if Esther was there, would Faith ever tell Mandie her problem?

4

Joe's Suggestion

WHEN THE SCHOOL BELL rang that afternoon for dismissal, Mandie rushed to get her coat and tam. Joe and Faith were right behind her. Esther pushed her way through the other students to catch up with them. Mandie sighed. She had been hoping Esther would change her mind about walking with them to Miss Abigail's.

"Once I learn all that fancy needlework, I'll be able to make all kinds of nice things for myself," Esther said, walking down the dusty road beside Mandie.

Mandie was shocked. "Things for yourself? But we're learning all this so we can take care of Mrs. Chapman's orders while she's gone," she said. "That's the way she makes her living, you know."

"But I may not have time to do any work for Mrs. Chapman," Esther argued. "I want to make some things for myself."

"Esther, if you're not going to help Mrs. Chapman, then I don't think you ought to join us," Mandie told her.

"What difference does it make what I do?" Esther was beginning to grow angry. "If Miss Abigail is going to teach these things, I see no reason why I can't learn too." She turned up her nose. "For whatever purpose."

"That's all right," Faith said. "If you want to learn, I'm sure Miss Abigail will be glad to teach you. It's up to you to decide how you will use the knowledge."

Esther shrugged.

"I sure am glad I'm a boy and I don't have to learn all that fancy stuff," Joe said. "Come on, girls. We need to walk faster so I won't be late getting home. Let's get a move on."

Miss Abigail answered the door.

"I'm sorry, Miss Abigail, but I have to go straight on home," Mandie said. "We're not supposed to take time to come in."

"I understand," Miss Abigail said, stepping

out onto the porch with them. "But you must come back whenever you have time to visit, all of you." She looked from Mandie to Joe to Esther.

"Miss Abigail, I can't come in either, but I wanted to ask if you would allow me to join your group to learn needlework, please, ma'am," Esther said, turning on her best smile.

"I'm not sure what hours we will be keeping yet, Esther," Miss Abigail said. "We may work while y'all are in school."

Mandie spoke up. "I want to learn too, if you don't teach during school hours. My mother has already given me permission."

"My mother gave me permission also. She can't help because she has arthritis in her hands," Esther said, putting on a sad expression.

"It's too bad you young people want to learn and help out and the hours will be wrong for y'all to do that," Miss Abigail said thoughtfully. "I wish there was a way we could handle this."

Mandie had a sudden idea. "Miss Abigail, what if you came to our school once a week and taught us there?"

"Come to your school?" Miss Abigail repeated in surprise.

"Yes, ma'am," Mandie replied. "I believe Mr. Tallant would agree to it. We have study periods at various times while other groups are learning their lessons, and the ones who are interested could just join in with you."

"That sounds like a bright idea, but I'm not sure it would work out," Miss Abigail said slowly.

Then Joe had an idea. "Why don't you girls see if you could leave early one afternoon and come to Miss Abigail's for the needlework? Mr. Tallant might even be willing to give you school credit for that," he suggested.

"That's a better idea," Mandie agreed.

"Yes, that might work out," Miss Abigail said. "I couldn't go off to school and leave the ladies, but you girls could come here and join in. Yes, I believe that's the proper way to handle this needlework. What do you girls think?"

"Yes," Esther replied. "I could do that."

"That would be perfect," Mandie said. "Of course, I'll have to talk to my mother about it to be sure she agrees."

"Well, now that that's settled, Mandie, we'd better get on home," Joe reminded her.

"I'll see you at school tomorrow," Mandie told Faith. "Sooner or later we'll get time to sit down and talk. Don't give up."

"Thanks, Mandie," Faith replied with a little smile. "I'll see you tomorrow." Then, turning to Esther, she added, "And I'll see you at school tomorrow, Esther."

"Yes, well, I've got to get home too," Esther answered. "Thank you, Miss Abigail. I'll let you know what my mother says."

"And of course I'll have to discuss it with Mr. Tallant," Miss Abigail said. "Y'all come back now, you hear?"

Esther lived in the opposite direction, so she left them when they reached the road. Mandie and Joe went on toward Mandie's house.

"I'm glad you thought of us getting out of school early," Mandie told Joe as they walked. "I just hope Mr. Tallant and my mother will say it's all right."

Joe's brown eyes sparkled. "I can solve some things sometimes, can't I?"

"I've never said you couldn't," Mandie told him. "If we can arrange things like you suggested, just think, you would only have to walk home with me four days a week, not five." She gave him a teasing look.

"Now, Mandie, I don't *have* to walk home with you at all," Joe replied with a frown. "It's just become a habit ever since I walked you home on your first day of school. You seemed so little and so lost."

"But I'm not so little and lost now. I'm nine years old, remember," Mandie replied. "Anyhow, since we are the only two who live in this direction, I'm glad we can walk together. I'll be worried about you walking home by yourself on the day we go to Miss Abigail's." She grinned up at him.

"Don't worry about that. I'll probably get home much faster," Joe told her. He hurried on down the road, and Mandie rushed to keep up with him.

"I think Esther is selfish, and I might just tell her so when I get the chance," Mandie said, remembering the girl's words.

"Oh, no, now wait a minute," Joe said, slowing down a little. "I wouldn't do that if I were you. Esther can do spiteful things to people who cross her. The best way to handle her is to just ignore her."

"We-l-l." Mandie drew out the word. "I suppose you're right. But I still think she's selfish." Her face clouded over. "You know I still haven't had a chance to talk to Faith about whatever is bothering her."

"You're only guessing that something is bothering her. You don't know for sure. Mandie, you're always imagining things," Joe teased her.

"Well, most of the time what I imagine is real," Mandie replied.

The two had come to the lane leading down to the Shaws' house and stopped there. Joe handed Mandie her books.

"I'll see you in the morning," he told her, and turned to go back down the road.

"Let's go a little early and maybe I can catch Faith alone at school. She's always just about the first one there," Mandie said.

"All right, ten minutes early. Good night," Joe replied, walking off.

"Good night," Mandie called back to him as

she hurried down the pathway. She could see her father working on the split-rail fence he was putting up around the Shaws' property, and she decided to approach him first about the idea of getting out of school early one day a week to go to Miss Abigail's. He usually agreed with whatever she wanted.

Mr. Shaw saw her coming and stopped work to straighten up and wait for her. "And how is my little blue-eyes today? You look happy about something," he said as Mandie came to stand by the fence.

"Oh, I am happy," Mandie agreed. "I think we have figured out a way for us girls to help out with Mrs. Chapman's work."

She explained Joe's suggestion about leaving school early one day.

"That sounds like a pretty good idea, provided you don't let it interfere with your schoolwork," her father said. "And of course Mr. Tallant would have to arrange your schedule to take care of your studies."

"Oh, Daddy, thank you!" Mandie said excitedly. "Now I have to get Mama to agree."

"That may not be hard to do, since she will be at Miss Abigail's herself on the afternoon that you girls go there," her father reminded her.

"That's right," Mandie said. She hadn't thought about that. "I'll go ask her now and see what she has to say."

"I'll be inside in a little bit," her father called, picking up his hammer.

Mandie hurried on down to the house and entered through the back door, which opened into the kitchen. Mrs. Shaw was standing by the iron cookstove stirring the contents of a large steaming pot.

Mrs. Shaw glanced over at Mandie. "Get your homework done now, and if you have time you can set the table for supper."

"Yes, ma'am," Mandie said, taking off her coat and tam as she walked toward the doorway to the parlor, holding her books in her other hand. "I don't have much homework. I'll hurry, Mama."

Mandie stepped into the parlor, hung up her coat and tam on the pegs by the doorway, and took her books to a chair by the window. She had only one page of arithmetic problems and one chapter to read in her reading book.

"Have you seen Irene?" her mother asked, poking her head into the room.

Mandie looked up from her books. "No, ma'am. Joe and I walked with Faith to Miss Abigail's, and I suppose Irene came home by herself."

"I thought maybe she had gone with you and Joe," Mrs. Shaw replied.

"Do you want me to go ask Daddy if he's seen her?" Mandie asked.

"No, never mind, she'll probably be along anytime now," Mrs. Shaw replied, going back into the kitchen.

Mandie hurried through her homework and then went back to the kitchen to set the table for supper. Just then Irene came in the back door.

"Where did you go?" Irene asked. "I looked for you and Joe to walk home with me and I never did find y'all."

"Irene, you knew we were going by Miss Abigail's with Faith," Mandie reminded her.

"No, I didn't," Irene said, removing her coat and hat. "When you asked permission to walk home with Faith, you didn't say *when* you were going, so I didn't know you were going today." She hung her things on the pegs by Mandie's, tossed her books on a nearby chair in the parlor, and came back into the kitchen.

"I'm sorry, Irene," Mandie said. "I suppose I just plain forgot to tell you we were going today. Anyway, you disappeared when school let out."

Mandie walked over to the cabinet to get the dishes. Irene followed her across the room.

"I don't remember seeing you outside in the schoolyard," Irene told her, getting the silverware from the drawer in the cabinet.

"Now, now, let's stop this conversation right here and now," Mrs. Shaw told the girls. She began pouring the contents of the large pot into a bowl.

"Mama, we talked to Miss Abigail about arranging for us girls to help with the needlework," Mandie told her mother. She explained the suggestion that they leave school early one day to do it. "So you see, if we go one afternoon you'll probably be there too, won't you?"

Mrs. Shaw continued putting the food on the table, her long skirt swishing as she moved.

"I certainly am hungry. I believe I can eat half of that pot of beans you cooked there," Mr. Shaw said, coming in the back door. He began washing up at the dry sink.

"That wouldn't do. It would only leave the three of us one-third each of the other half," Mandie said teasingly. "I was just telling Mama about the idea of getting out of school early one afternoon a week, like I told you."

Mr. and Mrs. Shaw looked at each other. Mandie knew that each of them was waiting for the other to make a decision. Finally Mr. Shaw spoke. "I suppose it wouldn't hurt their homework if they came straight home and got that done, would it?"

" 'They'?" Irene repeated. "Don't count me in. I don't want to do that."

"Well, if you think it would work out, Jim, we could let Amanda try it," Mrs. Shaw said. Turning to Mandie, she added, "But mind you, if you don't get all your lessons done on time, that will be the end of the needlework, do you hear?"

Mandie smiled broadly. "Yes, ma'am. Thank you, Mama."

Now all that had to be done was to persuade Mr. Tallant to let the girls out of school early. If everything worked out, Mandie would have a chance to talk privately with Faith while she was at Miss Abigail's. She was determined to find out what Faith's problem was.

5

Lessons Begin

THE NEXT MORNING, which was Wednesday, Mr. Tallant did something surprising as soon as the bell rang.

"Please come to order," the schoolmaster said, tapping his pencil on his desk. "I have an announcement to make."

The murmurs rippling across the room came to a halt, and the pupils straightened up in their seats. Mandie waited to see what Mr. Tallant had to say. *Probably something about our lessons,* she thought.

"It has come to my attention that Miss Abigail Durham will begin holding needlework classes for the women of the community to assist Mrs. Chapman, who is in New York for medical treatment," Mr. Tallant began.

Mandie's heart beat faster. She looked at Joe and caught his eye. They exchanged smiles.

"It has also come to my attention that some of you young ladies would like to leave early one afternoon each week to join in the work," the schoolmaster continued. "Now, if these young ladies will stand so that I can see how many wish to do this, I would appreciate it." He looked around the room expectantly.

Mandie immediately stood up beside her desk and motioned for Faith to rise also, which she did. Then Esther jumped up.

"We have three. Is that all?" Mr. Tallant asked, looking around the room again.

No one else rose. "I understand the classes will begin this afternoon. You three will be dismissed as soon as recess is over. I was told you should eat before going because the lessons won't begin until one o'clock. Every Wednesday until I receive further notice, you will be permitted to leave early. Just don't let it interfere with your schoolwork. Now, let's get down to our regular business. Everyone rise and bow your heads for our morning prayer."

Everyone stood with Mr. Tallant and recited the daily prayer, which they all had memorized. "Dear God, we thank Thee for another wonderful day. Help us to make the most of it in honoring You and loving each other. Amen."

Mandie excitedly counted the hours until it would be time to go to Miss Abigail's. Finally she would be able to have a private conversation with Faith! Things were beginning to look up.

At noon recess Mandie was so excited she could hardly eat her biscuit. She sat on a log with Faith and Joe. Esther came over to join them, which she had never done before. Maybe Esther was trying to be a friend, Mandie decided.

"I just thought of something," Mandie told the others. "We never asked if we should bring any needles, thread, or cloth. Do y'all suppose we should?" She looked at the other two girls.

"I don't think so," Faith said, passing around her overloaded lunch basket for her friends to share.

Mandie and Joe both took a drumstick and thanked her. Esther looked curiously at Faith. "Are you giving away all your food?"

"Oh, no, there's more than I can eat," Faith explained. "Please take some." She held the basket in front of the girl.

Esther hesitated and then removed a piece of chicken. "Thank you," she said. "This will be much better than the biscuits I brought."

"I'm afraid Miss Dicey doesn't realize I can't eat all the food she puts in my lunch basket every day," Faith said, taking out a piece of chicken for herself. "In case y'all are wondering about the quick permission for us to leave early, Mr. Tallant stopped by Miss Abigail's house last night with a book she had loaned him. She invited him to stay for tea and told him about our plans."

"So Mr. Tallant has been having tea with Miss Abigail?" Esther said, grinning at her friends.

Not one to gossip, Mandie said, "I'm glad we're going to get started at the very beginning of the classes." Turning to Joe, she added, "And I still have a chance to go with the men on Friday and Saturday afternoons."

Joe sighed. "Maybe, but you'll have to get permission from your father."

"I know," Mandie replied. She got a glimpse of her sister sitting with Tommy Lester across the yard. Irene was not going to like being left to do all the chores at home.

"You're planning to work with the men?" Esther asked in surprise.

"If my father allows it, I'll serve the food for them while they work," Mandie explained.

"Well, I hope that's all you're going to do," Esther said. "It wouldn't be very ladylike to join in the men's work." She made a face.

"Oh, Mandie is not very ladylike anyhow, sometimes," Joe teased.

"Well, who wants to be a stuffy old lady all the time? I sure don't," Mandie said. "But then, I'm not being brought up with all the ladylike things you are accustomed to, Esther. Our family doesn't have money like yours for hired help around the house and on the farm."

Esther tightened her thin lips. "You can be ladylike without being rich."

"And you can be rich without being ladylike," Faith quipped.

"Well, now that we're even, let's change the subject," Joe said. "We'll probably get mail from my father any day now to let us know when he's coming home, Faith, and whether your grandmother will be staying in New York for treatment. I'll come straight over and let you know when we hear."

"Thank you, Joe," Faith said with a slight smile. "Grandmother will write if she is to stay in New York, but your father will know more about what's going on with the doctors."

Mandie took Faith's hand and squeezed it. "I hope your grandmother has to stay awhile in New York, because that will mean the doctors up there think they can help her."

"So do I," Esther added.

"Thanks," Faith said as her eyes filled with tears. She obviously missed her grandmother very much.

The bell suddenly clanged to end recess, and everyone scrambled back to the schoolhouse. The three girls rushed to get their coats and hats and books and hurried back outside. It took them only a few minutes to get to Miss Abigail's house.

"Looks like everyone is here," Mandie remarked as she saw the Woodards' buggy and several carts and horses around the yard. Miss Dicey answered the door and let them in.

The women were in the large sitting room at the back of the house. Chairs were lined up along the wall. Miss Abigail bustled about. Mandie's mother sat chatting with Mrs. Woodard. They waved at Mandie.

"Now that we are all here, let's begin," Miss Abigail said, smiling at the girls. "Y'all just take a seat wherever you find one."

After asking questions and determining the extent of needlework knowledge that each person had, Miss Abigail divided them into groups: beginners, intermediates, and experts. Mandie, Faith, and Esther were among the beginners, along with two other young women who had come down from the mountain to help out.

After setting the others to work, Miss Abigail began with Mandie's group. "The first thing you need to learn is how to make tiny, dainty, even stitches, all in a row." She looked at Faith. "But, Faith, you shouldn't be in this group. You already know all this."

"I know, but I'd like to stay with my friends. Maybe I can help them," Faith replied.

"That's fine. In fact, that will help me tremendously. I can just give you the gist of what to teach them and you can supervise for me," Miss Abigail said with a smile.

"Thank you, Miss Abigail," Faith said happily.

So the beginners' group got off to a good start. Faith ended up teaching her friends and the two young women, and Miss Abigail took care of the others.

In the middle of the afternoon, Miss Abigail declared, "Ladies, we will take a break now for tea."

Faith stood up. "I'll help Miss Dicey serve the tea, Miss Abigail."

"Thank you, Faith, that is awfully sweet of you," Miss Abigail said.

Mandie stood up. "And I'll help you, Faith." Before anyone could say anything, she followed Faith out of the room, down the long hallway, and into the kitchen, where Miss Dicey was arranging small cakes on a silver platter.

"What can I do to help?" Mandie asked Miss Dicey.

"My, my, I do have lots of help, don't I?" Miss Dicey said, picking up a tablecloth from a cabinet nearby. "I'll just go lay the tablecloth if you girls will get the teapot and things out of the china closet in the hallway."

"Sure, Miss Dicey," Mandie replied, turning back to the doorway. "Do you know what to get from the china closet?" she asked Faith. She stood aside and allowed Faith to lead the way to the cabinet.

"I think I do," Faith replied.

There was a key in the lock on the china cabinet's door, but it was unlocked. Faith opened the glass door and paused.

"I'm not sure how many cups and saucers to get, are you?" she asked Mandie.

Mandie thought for a moment. "Let's just take out a dozen, and if that's not enough we can come back for more."

The girls carefully carried the china to the kitchen for Miss Dicey to put on the huge silver serving trays. Miss Dicey looked over what they had brought. "Now I will need that large teapot in the corner in the cabinet. Please be very careful with it. It belonged to Miss Abigail's great-grandmother."

"Yes, ma'am," Faith replied.

The two went back to the cabinet.

"I don't see any large teapot in the corner, do you?" Mandie asked Faith as they surveyed the contents.

Faith frowned and shook her head. She reached for a large teapot with blue flowers that rested on another shelf. "This one will probably do just as well," she said.

When they got back to the kitchen, Miss Dicey looked at the teapot. "That's not the right one, but I don't suppose it matters. We'll use it." She took the teapot and finished arranging one of the silver trays.

As Faith started back to join the women, Mandie stopped her in the hallway. "Faith, please tell me what's wrong. We could talk a minute without anyone hearing us."

Faith wouldn't look at Mandie. "Nothing's wrong. It's just that I don't know what to do about something that could be important."

"Well, if it's something that's important, tell me what it is," Mandie told her. "Maybe I *can* help, or at least try."

Faith hung her head. Mandie was becoming worried. Something was definitely wrong.

"Please, Faith, let me see if I can help," she urged.

At that moment Miss Dicey came hurrying through with the tray. "Watch out, young ladies, we don't want to spill the tea," she said with a laugh.

The girls stepped to the side as Miss Dicey passed through. Then Faith started walking after her. "We'd better get back or Miss Abigail may wonder what happened to us," she told Mandie over her shoulder.

Just as the two entered the sitting room, Miss Abigail told Miss Dicey, "But that's the wrong teapot. Did you not see the matching one? The one with the rosebuds?"

"This is the one the girls brought to the kitchen for me, and I decided not to bother going back for the other one," Miss Dicey answered.

"Well, all right for this time," Miss Abigail said. "Now, if you'll please pour the tea for me, I'll pass the sweet cakes."

Mandie hadn't realized Miss Abigail could be so picky about such things. Next time she would look for matching pieces of china so that she would meet with Miss Abigail's approval.

After tea, the afternoon seemed to fly by, and soon it was time to go home. Mrs. Shaw motioned for Mandie to join her.

"Come along, Amanda. Mrs. Woodard was good enough to bring me, and she will take us back home," Mrs. Shaw said.

"Faith, why don't you come over to visit me tomorrow after school?" Mandie asked. "We could do our homework together if you'd get permission from Miss Abigail. Then my father could bring you home later."

Faith's eyes lit up. "That would be nice. I'll ask Miss Abigail and let you know at school tomorrow."

Esther stood fidgeting near Faith. "Would you girls mind if I come along too?"

Mandie paused. "Of course not. Come with us if you like."

"Esther, how are you going to get home?" Faith asked.

"Mrs. Clark will take me," Esther said, motioning toward an elderly woman with fluffy white hair who stood across the room. "She lives just down the hill from us, so it won't be out of her way. See y'all tomorrow." She went to join Mrs. Clark.

"Seems like we never get a chance to talk alone, do we?" Mandie said to Faith as she put on her coat.

Faith laughed. "You're too popular, that's what it is. And if we're doing this tomorrow after school, you might as well ask Joe, too, since he always walks home with you."

"That's a good idea," Mandie replied with a smile. "We'll just have our own afternoon, then."

When Mandie got home with her mother, she found her father setting the table.

"Hope y'all made some progress on your needlework," he remarked as he smiled at Mandie and his wife.

"We did," Mrs. Shaw said, removing her wraps.

"It'll take time, but we'll learn," Mandie added, also taking off her coat and tam.

"Where is Irene?" Mrs. Shaw asked. "Did she come straight home from school this afternoon?"

"Yes, but I gave her permission to walk over to Tommy Lester's house with some of those apples we've got there in the pantry. They're beginning to get soft."

"Well, I hope she gets back in time for supper," Mrs. Shaw said.

Windy came from behind the warm cookstove and followed Mandie as she put her coat and tam on the pegs beside her mother's. Mandie picked Windy up and nuzzled the fur beneath her neck.

"Amanda, don't get cat hairs flying everywhere now. The food is being put on the table," Mrs. Shaw scolded.

Mandie set the kitten down. "Yes, ma'am. I'll wash up." She went to the washpan in the dry sink, poured clean water into it, and washed her face and hands.

"Before I forget, Mama, I asked Faith to come home from school with me tomorrow so we could do our homework together. And Esther wants to come too, and then Faith suggested I ask Joe, so I hope it's all right."

"Of course it's all right," Mrs. Shaw said with a smile. "Your friends are welcome anytime."

"And, you know, Faith said something in the

hallway to me at Miss Abigail's about something important, but we didn't get a chance to talk any more. That's the reason I asked her here tomorrow, but now Esther is tagging along," Mandie explained. The situation was so frustrating!

"I believe I can help out on that," Mr. Shaw said, turning from the stove. "I'll take Esther home first and then you can talk all you want with Faith."

"Oh, Daddy, thanks!" Mandie exclaimed. She thought now she might be able to discuss things with Faith at last. This was a good thing, because her patience was running out!

6
More Mystery

THE NEXT MORNING the temperature turned much colder at Charley Gap. Even though the Shaws' home was nestled down in the hollow between the mountains, strong gusts of cold wind managed to rattle the windowpanes and wake Mandie. She sat up to look outside. The sun was beginning to shine, but the light was weak and thin.

"Br-r-r-r!" Mandie whispered to herself, sliding back down under the warm, heavy quilts. Then she heard the clink of the stove lid downstairs, and she knew her father must be up and stoking the fire in the cookstove, which was never allowed to go out in the winter months. The stove heated the whole house, but best of all, the heat rose to the attic room she shared with her sister and it was never really cold.

The aroma of perking coffee reached the attic, and Mandie sat up again. "Might as well get up. Coffee's done," she whispered as she looked across at her sister, still soundly sleeping.

Rushing across the room barefooted, Mandie pulled down a warm navy-blue dress from the small closet under the eaves. She grabbed clean stockings and her shoes, hurried back to her bed, and got dressed. Brushing back her hair, she plaited it into a long braid and tied the end of it with a white ribbon.

Quietly descending the ladder into the parlor, Mandie picked up her schoolbooks to check her homework. She wanted to be sure she hadn't made any mistakes. She'd been told by everyone involved that the needlework couldn't interfere with her schoolwork.

"That looks all right," she said to herself as she scanned the arithmetic assignment and then looked over her spelling. "And so does that." She closed her books and put them back on the table.

"I thought I heard someone," her father said from the doorway into the kitchen. "Good morning."

"Good morning, Daddy, but you know I don't believe it *is* going to be a good morning," Mandie replied as she followed her father into the kitchen. "It looks awfully cold out there." She went to cuddle Windy, who had come out from under the warm cookstove.

"*Looks* awfully cold? But, now, I thought cold was something you feel," her father teased as he poured two cups of coffee, one for him and one for her, and brought them to the table.

Mandie sat down with her father to drink the hot coffee. "But when the wind is blowing as hard as it is now, wouldn't you say it looks cold?" she asked, frowning.

"That's because you know it's winter and the wind is bound to be cold," Mr. Shaw said with a twinkle in his eyes.

"I just hope it isn't too cold for my friends to come over after school today," Mandie told him.

"I'll tell you what," Mr. Shaw said. "Why don't I just take the wagon and pick you all up from school?"

"Oh, would you?" Mandie exclaimed. "That would save us time, too, because we would get home faster, and then we would have more time together. Thank you, Daddy."

"Then that's what we'll do," Mr. Shaw replied.

And that was what they did. When school let out, Mr. Shaw was waiting on the road in his wagon. Faith, Esther, and Joe all came home with the Shaws. Mandie's mother had hot cocoa waiting, and the young people gathered around the kitchen table.

"I don't think it's going to be hard to learn all those fancy stitches," Esther remarked, taking out her pencil.

"I enjoyed being in Miss Abigail's house with all her pretty things," Mandie said.

"But what about her making a fuss about that silly old teapot because Miss Dicey brought the wrong one? After all, a teapot is a tea-pot, no matter what color or shape it is," Esther said.

"I don't think there was a teapot in the china cabinet that matched the cups and saucers," Mandie said.

"On the way home Mrs. Clark told me she has been in Miss Abigail's house lots of times and had tea from that blue-flowered teapot served in blue-flowered teacups," Esther said.

"But we didn't use the blue-flowered cups and saucers. We took the ones with the tiny pink rosebuds on them," Mandie said. "So I suppose we mixed everything up."

"Yes," Faith agreed.

"Did Miss Abigail find the missing teapot when Miss Dicey cleaned everything up after all the visitors left?" Joe asked Faith.

"No, I don't think she did," Faith replied. Taking a deep breath, she asked, "Don't y'all think we should get busy with our homework?"

"Good idea," Joe agreed.

"I was at Miss Abigail's with my mother and a lot of other people for tea the day before Faith moved in," Esther said. "And I don't remember for sure, but I don't believe Miss Abigail had such a teapot in her china cabinet. I was looking at all the dishes, and I don't remember seeing a teapot with pink roses on it."

"You were handling all that expensive china and crystal in Miss Abigail's cabinet?" Mandie asked in surprise. "Suppose you had broken something? What would you have done?"

"Oh, she probably wouldn't miss anything if someone did break a piece," Esther said. "She never uses all of it. The only reason she missed the teapot was because you and Faith happened to get out the cups and saucers that match it. She usually uses the blue-flowered dishes," she added importantly.

Mandie suddenly had a thought. Had Esther taken out the pink-flowered teapot and broken it while she was going through the things in the cabinet? Of course, if Esther had, she would never in this world admit it.

When they had finished their lessons, Joe stood up and announced that he had better get going. "It's getting late and will soon be time for supper," he told the girls as he packed up his books and papers. Faith and Esther followed suit.

"Don't y'all remember?" Mandie asked. "My father said he would take everyone home. I'll see where he is." As she started for the door to the parlor, her father came in the back door. She stopped. "Daddy, they're all ready to go home."

"All right now, let's see," he replied. "Since Esther lives in a different direction, let's drop her off first, and then we'll pass by the Woodards' and leave Joe, and Faith will be last. That way we don't have to backtrack. Is that acceptable to everyone?"

"Yes, sir," the group chorused.

Mandie had never been to Esther's house. When she saw it she understood why the girl evidently thought she was better than most of the other young people in the community.

"Thank you, Mr. Shaw," Esther said as Mandie's father pulled the wagon to a stop in the horseshoe-shaped driveway. "Goodbye," she told her friends as she hopped down.

Mandie gazed at the huge two-story, brown-shingled house. Lace curtains hung in the windows, and shrubbery was planted around the porch. The yard was manicured and neat—the grass was not allowed to grow naturally as other people's grass was in Charley Gap. *Esther's family must have lots of money*, Mandie thought, *maybe as much as Miss Abigail.*

Mr. Shaw dropped Joe off next. Mandie and Faith sat in the back of the wagon, and Mandie spoke in a low voice. "Faith, now we can talk a little bit without all those other people around," she said. "My father can't hear us over the noise of the wagon and the horse."

Faith looked shyly at her. "I enjoyed my afternoon at your house. Now you'll have to come to Miss Abigail's and do homework with me one afternoon soon."

"You heard Esther talking about going through Miss Abigail's china cabinet," Mandie said. "Do you think she might have taken out the teapot and broken it?"

Faith fidgeted with her books. "I'm sorry, Mandie, but I can't accuse someone of doing wrong if I don't know for sure they did it. Esther is so loud and talkative, she might say or do anything."

"I agree," Mandie said, holding on to the side of the wagon as they drove down the rutted road. "Faith, you wanted to talk to me. You've been saying you were worried about something, but someone always interrupts us. No one can hear us now. Do you want to tell me what it is?"

Faith looked down at her lap. "It's just that I seem to have so many problems, and Ma is not here to talk to about them. In fact, most of the problems wouldn't even exist if I were home with my grandmother."

"Problems like what?" Mandie asked.

"Oh, you know," Faith said vaguely. "I don't really know Miss Abigail, and even though she's awfully nice, I'm just not comfortable around her. She . . ." She paused.

"I understand what you're saying, Faith, but you'll get better acquainted with Miss Abigail, and I know you'll love her. Everyone does," Mandie assured her. "You said you had a problem of some kind. Could I help?"

"I just can't talk about it right now," Faith told her. "I would rather wait and discuss it with my grandmother when she comes back home."

"But, Faith, your grandmother may not be back for a long time yet," Mandie reminded her. "If you want to tell me about it, I certainly won't tell anyone else. It might help for you to share the problem with me."

"I know, Mandie, but I—I . . ." Faith broke off. "Not right now, please." She turned her head to look out at the road.

* * *

The next day at school, Mr. Tallant announced that since it was Friday and the men would begin work on Mrs. Chapman's place, school would be closed early.

"We'll go home immediately after noon recess today," the schoolmaster said. "Since all of you have brought your lunches, eat first, because food cannot be wasted, and then the boys who would like to may go and help. I understand from Miss Abigail that she may have another sewing session in mind this afternoon. Since most of us will be working this weekend, we will not have any homework."

"Thank you, Mr. Tallant!" Excited smiles lit up the room.

"However, you will all have to really knuckle down and study hard in class every day. We can't get behind with our work," Mr. Tallant told them.

Mandie smiled over at Faith. Then Esther caught her eye.

"I want to go with y'all to Miss Abigail's today," Esther whispered.

Mandie shrugged. "If you like." The way

things were going, Faith probably wouldn't want to talk anyway.

When the girls arrived at Miss Abigail's, they found a lot more women there than on the previous day. Mandie scanned the room for her mother.

"Do you know if my mother is planning to come this afternoon?" Mandie asked as Miss Abigail was showing people to chairs in the sitting room.

"No, dear, she is not," Miss Abigail whispered. "And Mrs. Woodard is at your house. You know what they are doing." She smiled.

Mandie was puzzled for a moment, and then it dawned on her. Her mother and Mrs. Woodard were working on dresses for Faith! She glanced at Faith's thin, worn cotton dress. Faith would be thrilled!

When it came time for tea that afternoon, Mandie noticed that Faith did not volunteer to help Miss Dicey. However, Esther stood right up.

"I will go help Miss Dicey," Esther told Miss

Abigail as she began walking across the room toward the hallway.

"Thank you, dear," Miss Abigail said as Esther disappeared through the doorway.

And when Miss Dicey served tea, all the cups and plates were blue-flowered. Esther, following Miss Dicey back into the room and carrying the teapot on a silver tray, glanced at it, then looked at Mandie and Faith and smiled. The teapot was blue-flowered.

"I suppose Esther was afraid to get out the pink-flowered dishes for fear the teapot was still missing," Mandie whispered to Faith.

Faith fiddled with the needlework in her lap and nodded. "She should be very careful, because if anything were broken Miss Abigail wouldn't like it," she whispered in reply.

Mandie nodded and bent closer. "Would you like to come with me tomorrow to help serve the food to the men who will be working on your house?" she asked. "Please don't say anything in front of Esther," she quickly added. "I don't think she would want to go anyway, but you can never tell about her."

Faith smiled faintly. "I'll have to get Miss Abigail's permission, but I'm sure she'll agree. I'll try to ask her before you leave today."

Esther worked her way through the crowded room and came back to sit by Mandie and Faith.

"You see, I matched up all the dishes," she told them proudly.

"Yes, you did a good job," Faith agreed. "I'm glad I didn't have to handle those expensive dishes."

"They're only dishes that money bought, and money can buy more," Esther said with a shrug.

"But it would take a lot of money to replace those dishes," Mandie replied.

"Are you going with the men tomorrow, Mandie?" Esther asked.

"I'm not sure right now," Mandie replied.

"Well, I'm sure I'm *not* going and get all cold and dirty," Esther said.

Mandie looked at Faith and smiled.

7

Evidence

MISS ABIGAIL HAD given permission for Faith to go with Mandie and help serve the food on Saturday. The day was warmer and the sun was shining brightly. On their way, Mandie and her father stopped by and picked up Faith.

Although Mandie was unable to get Faith to talk about what was troubling her, the girls enjoyed serving the food for the men and then helping Joe clean the yard. And when the day ended, Faith seemed happier and more talkative than she'd been since her grandmother had gone to New York.

"I really enjoyed the day with y'all," Faith told Mr. Shaw on the drive home.

"I'm glad you did," Mr. Shaw said. "And you are welcome to come back again. We men will be doing more work next weekend."

"Thank you, sir," Faith said. "I hope I can." Turning to Mandie, she asked, "Do you think you would be able to come to Miss Abigail's Monday afternoon?"

"I'd love to if I have permission," Mandie said, looking up at her father.

"Sure," he said. "I'll come and bring you home after y'all are finished with your homework. We won't be working on Mrs. Chapman's house Monday."

"Thanks, Daddy," Mandie said. "We'll plan on it," she said happily to Faith.

On Monday afternoon Mandie and Faith walked to Miss Abigail's house to do their homework.

Miss Abigail, always the perfect hostess, insisted they should take a break for tea in the middle of the afternoon.

"No need to help me," Miss Dicey insisted as she left the room to make preparations. "There are only two of you today."

Mandie watched everything and saw that Miss Dicey used the blue-flowered dishes. Mandie wondered again if anyone had found the missing teapot but was afraid to ask, for fear it might upset Miss Abigail.

"I have an errand to run and will be back shortly," Miss Abigail said, coming into the room with her coat and hat on. "I'm glad you could come, Amanda, and you must make this a regular habit, visiting here."

"Thank you, Miss Abigail. I'll come back again when my mother allows it," Mandie told her.

As soon as Miss Abigail had left, Faith asked Mandie, "Would you like to see some of the needlework my grandmother and I do for other people?"

"Oh, yes, I would," Mandie answered.

"Come on, then. I have some of it in my room. I try to keep all my personal things in the room that Miss Abigail gave me so I won't clutter up her beautiful house," Faith remarked as she led Mandie into the hallway.

The girls passed the china closet on their way to the staircase. Mandie paused to glance through the glass doors at the beautiful china and crystal.

"All this is so wonderful to have!" Mandie exclaimed as she moved closer to the cabinet to peer inside at the dishes in the back.

"Yes, it is," Faith agreed, stopping at the foot of the steps to wait.

Mandie had started to move toward the stairs when the toe of her shoe hit something under the edge of the cabinet. She frowned down at the cabinet's legs. *What was that?* She slid the toe of her shoe along the floor. To her amazement, a piece of broken china came out from under the cabinet. She quickly stooped and picked it up. There were pink roses on it!

"Faith!" Mandie exclaimed breathlessly as she turned the broken china over in her hand. "Look!"

Faith hurried back to her side and looked at the piece without saying a word.

"Do you think it could be a piece of the missing teapot?" Mandie asked. Then she thought: Had Esther broken the teapot and hidden the pieces? Or . . . could it have been Faith?

Faith nodded. "Maybe." Then, looking at Mandie, she asked, "What are you going to do with it?"

Mandie thought for a moment. "I suppose I should give it to Miss Abigail. What do you think?"

Faith seemed to have lost her voice. She stammered, "I—I—I just don't know. It—it w-would upset her something aw-awful."

"But she ought to know. It was her teapot," Mandie said.

"Why don't we just put it away somewhere safe and look for the rest of it before we mention it to Miss Abigail?" Faith said, her voice unsteady.

Mandie was trying to decide whether Faith was guilty. Maybe they did need to hide this piece until the person who broke it could be found. But how were they going to figure out who broke it if it wasn't Faith?

"Where could we put this piece so it will be safe until we can look for the rest of the teapot?" Mandie finally asked.

"In my room," Faith quickly told her. "I clean my own room and no one else ever goes in, so it will be safe there. Come on." She turned and started up the staircase.

Upstairs, Faith led Mandie into her room, and Mandie's blue eyes leaped with joy at the beautiful furnishings. Everything was pink and white. Even the wallpaper had pink rosebuds floating down the walls. The four-poster bed had a ruffled canopy with lacy pink rosebuds drooping off the edge.

"Oh, it's so beautiful I can't find words for it!" Mandie said with a loud sigh. "Do you have all pink-and-white dreams sleeping in this room?" She grinned at her friend.

Faith laughed. "Not exactly," she said, loosening up. "But it is a comfortable bed." Her face turned sober. "And I do appreciate Miss Abigail's having me stay here while my grandmother is gone."

Mandie looked at the piece of china in her hand. "Now, where can we put this?" She held it out to Faith.

Faith looked around the room. "In that cushion on the window seat over there." She went over to the double windows, where a window seat had been built in, and picked up one of the cushions. "There."

Mandie placed the broken piece of china on the window seat, and Faith covered it with the cushion and then patted it. "There now," she said. "It will be safe there."

Mandie thought about Esther. "Faith, do you remember Esther told us she had been looking through the dishes in the china cabinet the day before you came to stay here?" she asked. "Do you think she could have broken the teapot then?"

Faith frowned. "I—I—I just don't know," she replied in a low, shaky voice.

"Faith, I'm not accusing anyone of breaking the teapot." Mandie took a deep breath. "You know, I have a special verse I say when I'm in trouble or afraid of consequences. If I say 'What time I am afraid I will put my trust in Thee,' it helps me feel better."

Faith slowly repeated the verse. " 'What time I am afraid I will put my trust in Thee.' That's a good verse to know."

"Also when I'm afraid of admitting wrong-doings, I've found it's much worse not to admit things and then be found out later," Mandie told her. "The consequences are always more severe for not owning up about it in the first place."

Faith looked at Mandie with a sad expression on her face. But she didn't say anything.

"I think we should talk to Esther and tell her we found a piece of the teapot," Mandie declared. "Then if she did it, maybe she would confess."

"Oh, I don't know about that," Faith answered. "Esther might think we're accusing her."

"But we won't be accusing her," Mandie insisted. "We'll just tell her that we know the teapot was broken because we have found a piece of it. And we could see how she reacts."

"But she has already said it was just an old teapot and money could buy another one," Faith argued.

"The fact that the teapot was missing didn't seem to bother her much. If she was the one who broke it, she might just think 'So what?' and confess," Mandie said, trying to decide whether Faith was guilty or not.

"I doubt that Esther would confess to any wrongdoing," Faith said. "Why don't we wait and see if we can find the rest of the teapot?"

"It would be awfully hard for us to search Miss Abigail's house," Mandie said. "Miss Abigail is home almost all the time, and she would wonder what we were up to."

"We could figure out a way," Faith said.

There was the sound of a horse and wagon outside. Mandie went to look out the window. Her father had pulled up in front of the house.

"There's my father. I have to go now, Faith," Mandie said, starting toward the door to the hall. She stopped to look back. "Now that we have a piece of the teapot, we really should solve this mystery."

"We will, we will," Faith hurriedly told her. "Let's not keep your father waiting, now."

Mandie couldn't figure out whether Faith was really interested in solving the mystery or whether she just wanted Mandie to leave quickly.

When they got downstairs, Mandie put on her coat and tam, grabbed her books, and then turned to Faith, who seemed to be rushing her out the front door. "Think about Esther," Mandie said. "Let me know what you think we should do: whether we ought to tell her about the piece we found, or maybe just give her a hint that we know something. We could talk at recess tomorrow."

"But recess is not very private," Faith objected as she opened the front door and stood waiting for Mandie to leave.

"We can get away from the others, except for Joe," Mandie told her. "I always tell him everything anyway. He never tells. In fact, he might help us decide whether Esther is guilty or not if we talk to her in front of him."

"Let's discuss it tomorrow," Faith said. She pointed to the road. "Your father is waiting, Mandie."

"I know," Mandie replied, still wondering what the big hurry was about. She went out onto the porch and started down the steps. Then she turned back. "Maybe I should tell my father. He might know what to do."

"Oh, no, not your father!" Faith quickly replied. "Don't talk to him about it, please!"

Mandie was surprised at this request but didn't reply. She hurried on out to the wagon. As she climbed in, she looked back, but Faith had already gone inside the house and closed the door.

"I wonder," Mandie said under her breath as she joined her father on the seat.

"You wonder?" Mr. Shaw asked as he shook the reins to start the horse down the road.

"Oh, did you hear that? I was talking to myself,"

Mandie said with a big grin. Her father really had good ears.

"Your mother and Mrs. Woodard have just about finished two dresses for Faith, I believe," her father told her as they drove.

"They have?" Mandie asked excitedly. She could hardly wait to see the expression on Faith's face when they gave her the new clothes.

"Yes, and they look mighty pretty to me," her father added.

Mandie looked up at her father as they rode along. "Daddy, if you knew someone had done something bad, would you tell on them if they didn't confess after they had a chance to?" she asked thoughtfully.

Mr. Shaw cleared his throat. "That's a mighty complicated question, Amanda. I don't think you ought to tell on someone, unless you're positive they are guilty and they're causing a lot of trouble by not owning up. On the other hand, I don't think you should get involved in someone else's business." He looked down at her.

Mandie sighed loudly and shifted in her seat. "Well, I'll just have to explain, I suppose," she began. "You see, Miss Abigail has a set of expensive china that belonged to her great-grandmother, and the teapot is missing. I believe I know who broke it. I know it's broken because I found a piece of it at her house."

"Stop right there, Amanda," Mr. Shaw told his daughter. "You only believe you know; you aren't certain you know. And this sounds like something that does not concern you in any way. I'd say back away. Don't get involved in this."

Mandie was surprised because she thought her father always wanted to straighten out wrongs, but then, maybe he was right. It didn't really concern her.

"Well, it wouldn't hurt anything if I just observed everything and didn't say anything, would it?" she asked, frowning.

"That's the best way to handle it," her father said with a smile. "Don't cause trouble among your friends. They might not forgive you."

"All right, I won't get involved, then, but I will do a lot of thinking about it," Mandie said.

"That's my girl," Mr. Shaw said. With a big smile he added, "And I have some news that might better occupy your mind."

"Oh, really? What is it, Daddy?" Mandie replied, straightening up in her seat.

"The Woodards are planning a big get-together for the day Dr. Woodard returns home," he said.

"A party?" Mandie exclaimed. "When is he coming home? Were the doctors up there able to help Mrs. Chapman? Tell me, Daddy!"

"Not so fast, young lady, one question at a time," Mr. Shaw said, smiling. "Mrs. Woodard doesn't know yet when he will return, and according to what he wrote her, it is still uncertain whether the doctors can do anything for Mrs. Chapman. However, that will all be settled by the time he comes home."

"Oh, I hope he comes home without Mrs. Chapman," Mandie said quickly. "That would mean that she has to stay for treatment."

"Yes, that would be a blessing," Mr. Shaw said.

"Is it all right if I tell Faith about the get-together?" Mandie asked.

"I don't see any reason why not. I just hope she isn't disappointed if her grandmother returns with Dr. Woodard," he said.

Now Mandie had a little news that might

cheer up Faith. She couldn't wait until tomorrow at school to spread the word about the party. And she hoped and prayed the party would be without Mrs. Chapman. It was funny to think about—a party to celebrate a guest who wasn't even there!

Things are perking up a little, Mandie thought as her father turned the wagon into their lane and she remembered the new dresses for Faith.

8

Tying Up the Ends

THE NEXT DAY, which was Tuesday, Mandie was unable to speak with Faith until the noon break came. Then she hurried outside with Joe and motioned for Faith to follow.

"Come on, I have something to tell you," Mandie called back to her.

"All right," Faith replied, rushing to catch up.

As soon as Mandie sat down with Joe and Faith, Esther came to join them.

"I have some news," Mandie said, taking her biscuit out of her lunch basket. "Guess what? There's going to be a big party at the Woodards' when Dr. Woodard comes home, and—"

"Is my grandmother coming home with him?" Faith interrupted.

"When are they coming?" Esther asked.

Mandie looked at Joe.

"We don't know when my father is returning and we still don't know whether Mrs. Chapman will stay in New York," Joe explained. "But my mother says we'll have the get-together anyhow, whichever way it turns out, and if Mrs. Chapman doesn't come back with my father, then when she does come home, my mother will have another party just for her."

"Oh," Faith said quietly.

"Well, I for one hope we get to have two parties," Mandie said, looking at Faith.

Faith smiled. "Yes, I hope so too."

"So do I," Esther added.

Mandie wanted to tell Faith about the two new dresses, but she couldn't. She would have to wait for Miss Abigail to give them to Faith. However, Faith had seemed interested in the party, and that was what the group talked about for the rest of recess. The missing teapot was not mentioned.

Then on Wednesday it was time for another needlework lesson at Miss Abigail's. All the women attended who had been there before, and the three girls joined them.

Mrs. Woodard and Mrs. Shaw were late and

came in together. Mandie watched as Mrs. Woodard whispered something to Miss Abigail, who nodded at whatever was being said.

"Thank you," Miss Abigail told Mrs. Woodard, and then smiled over at Mrs. Shaw, who had sat down with the other women.

Mandie grinned. Her mother and Mrs. Woodard must have brought the dresses for Faith!

"What are you smiling at?" Esther asked Mandie.

Mandie looked innocently at her. "Oh, something I was just thinking about." And then she thought about the piece of broken china she had found. She couldn't resist the temptation to question Esther when Miss Dicey served tea that afternoon.

Before Miss Dicey got to the girls with the tea, Mandie asked Esther, "You said you didn't remember seeing the teapot with the pink roses when you went through the things in the china closet that day, the day before Faith moved in with Miss Abigail, didn't you?"

Esther blew out her breath. "Here we go again! That teapot!"

Mandie heard Faith inhale sharply beside her.

"The teapot still hasn't been found," Mandie said.

Esther jumped up. "Come on, I'll show you where the vacant spot was, the place where the teapot was supposed to have been sitting." She skipped across the room, and Mandie followed her out into the hallway. Faith came right behind them.

Esther stood in front of the china closet and pointed to a corner. "That's where that old teapot was supposed to be, and that's the same empty spot I saw that day," she said, her voice rising in anger.

Mandie glanced inside the glass door and asked, "How did you know the teapot was supposed to be there if you didn't know anything about the teapot then?"

"I didn't know about it then. I figured it out later, when y'all began talking about it," Esther told her. "I don't know why you're so interested in Miss Abigail's teapot. It didn't belong to you."

"Because I found—" Mandie stopped as she realized she was about to give away the fact that she had found the broken piece.

"You found what?" Esther asked, her eyes narrowing.

"Mandie!" Faith gasped.

"What did you find? Did you find that old teapot?" Esther demanded. "Is that what you're talking about? Is it?"

Mandie looked helplessly at Faith and reluctantly gave up on her promise not to discuss it. "Yes, I found a broken piece of china that must be part of the teapot," she said, closely watching Esther.

"What has that got to do with me?" Esther mumbled.

Mandie bit her lip and didn't reply. She was trying to decide if the girl was guilty.

"Are you accusing me of breaking that old teapot?" Esther continued loudly. "Are you?" She stepped up close to Mandie.

"No, no, no!" Faith suddenly began crying. "She didn't break it, Mandie. I did. I did it." She put her hands over her face.

At that moment Miss Abigail came rushing down the hallway toward them. "Girls!" she exclaimed, and tried to put an arm around Faith.

"I broke the teapot," Faith sobbed. "It was me. Your precious rosebud teapot!"

Miss Abigail attempted to pull the girl close. "Faith! No use crying over spilt milk, dear."

Faith kept her hands over her face. "I'm so sorry, Miss Abigail. I was only looking at it and it just fell."

"You are forgiven," Miss Abigail said, still trying to console her. But Faith kept pulling away.

"But, Faith, why were you interested in that old teapot, of all things?" Esther asked. "There are lots of pretty things in there, like the crystal bells and the silver candlestick holders. That was just an old teapot."

Faith tried to control her crying as she replied, "It—it looked just like—" She stopped to take a deep breath. "Just like one my grandmother had and it got burnt up when our house caught fire. It's gone too!" She began crying again.

Mandie was completely at a loss as to what to say or do. She had caused all this trouble, and she was afraid she had lost her friends because of it. Her father had warned her.

"Faith, I'm sorry," Mandie said, trying to touch the girl's hand. Faith yanked it away.

Miss Abigail tried again. "Faith, dear, I heard the whole conversation," she said. "I know you didn't break the teapot on purpose, and as much as I loved it, you are more important to me."

At that moment Miss Dicey came into the hallway. "Seems like I remember leaving hot cocoa in the kitchen, if there's anyone who would like to sample it," she said cheerfully. "Much better than tea any day, huh, girls?"

"Yes, ma'am," Mandie and Esther replied together.

"You girls go with Miss Dicey if you'd like hot cocoa," Miss Abigail told Mandie and Esther.

"Thank you, ma'am," Mandie said, hurrying toward the kitchen with Esther. But even the promise of delicious hot cocoa couldn't erase the sadness in Mandie's heart. Had she lost her new friend?

Suddenly Mandie looked back and saw Faith straighten up and look at Miss Dicey. Without a word, Miss Dicey held her arms out, and Faith ran to her. "Come along now, my child," Miss

Dicey said, putting her arm around Faith's shoulders and leading her toward the kitchen.

Then Miss Abigail smiled and started back toward the sitting room.

In the kitchen Miss Dicey filled three cups with hot cocoa and placed them before the girls at the table.

In a few moments the kitchen door opened and Mrs. Woodard, Mrs. Shaw, and Miss Abigail came into the room. Miss Abigail was carrying something covered with a white sheet.

"Faith, dear, we have a little present for you," Miss Abigail began. Mrs. Shaw and Mrs. Woodard helped her remove the sheet, revealing two beautiful dresses, one pink and one blue.

Faith's eyes widened with surprise.

Miss Abigail stepped closer to the girl and held up the dresses. "We hope these will fit."

Faith frowned in disbelief. "For me?"

"Yes, just for you. I furnished the material, and Mrs. Shaw and Mrs. Woodard made these just for you," Miss Abigail replied.

Faith clutched her cup of cocoa.

"Stand up, Faith, please, so we can see if we

got them the right length," Mrs. Woodard said, taking the pink dress and moving toward Faith.

Faith placed her cup on the table and stood up. Mrs. Woodard held the dress against her. "I believe it's perfect," she said. Pleased, she looked back at Mrs. Shaw.

"I thought she was the same height as Irene. I'm sure they'll fit," Mrs. Shaw said.

Faith looked at Miss Abigail, tears filling her eyes again. "But, Miss Abigail, why are you giving me these? I haven't done anything to deserve them."

"Oh, but you have, Faith," Miss Abigail told her, finally managing to put an arm around Faith. "You just don't know how much joy you have given me by living here with me. I've never had a daughter, but you're just like a daughter to me. I love you." She squeezed Faith's frail shoulders.

Faith threw her arms around Miss Abigail. "And I love you, Miss Abigail, for helping my grandmother to go to New York to see the doctors up there, and for giving me a home while she's gone."

Mrs. Woodard took the blue dress from Miss

Abigail and held both dresses up. "Now, tell me, Faith, which one will you be wearing to our get-together on Saturday?" she asked, smiling at the girl.

"Dr. Woodard is coming home!" Mandie exclaimed.

"Is my grandmother coming too?" Faith asked.

"I received a message from Dr. Woodard today, and he said he would definitely be home on Saturday because he has patients he needs to see, but he will not know until the last minute whether your grandmother will be staying in New York. The doctors have not given him their opinions yet," Mrs. Woodard explained.

"Of course, we are hoping your grandmother won't be with him," Mrs. Shaw added. Esther nodded.

Everyone was silent for a moment until Faith spoke. "Yes, we can have a party without my grandmother," she said. "In fact, that would be just fine. And if she doesn't come home, I'll wear the blue dress and save the pink one until she does get back, because she loves pink." Faith was excited as she turned to Mandie and Esther. "I've never had friends like this before."

Mandie blushed. "Oh, shucks, I think our hot cocoa is getting cold." She picked up her cup.

"And so is our tea," Miss Abigail said. "We'll just hang these dresses on the hall tree for you, dear, and you can take them up to your room when you're ready."

Faith finally smiled. "Thank you, Miss Abigail, and Mrs. Woodard and Mrs. Shaw. I really and truly appreciate the dresses."

"You're welcome, dear," Mrs. Woodard said.

"We're glad we could do this for you," Mrs. Shaw said.

As soon as the three ladies had left the kitchen, Faith twirled around in the middle of the floor. "Now I have four dresses!"

"And you probably will get more," Miss Dicey said from the stove, where she had been standing and listening to the conversation. "Now, y'all just drink that hot cocoa before it gets to be cold cocoa, you hear?"

Faith sat down.

"Faith, I'm sorry I caused all the trouble," Mandie apologized.

"Trouble? Mandie, I caused all the trouble by

not speaking up when I broke the teapot. I'm glad you brought everything out in the open. Now it's over with and I don't have a problem any longer," Faith told her.

Mandie grinned. "I'm glad, Faith."

"Now we have to wait and see if your grandmother comes home with Dr. Woodard," Esther said.

"Yes," Faith said.

There was no more word from Dr. Woodard. Mrs. Woodard asked everyone to come to her house Saturday morning and spend the entire day, not knowing what time her husband might return.

Miss Abigail and Faith picked up Esther and brought her with them. Mandie and her family arrived shortly afterward. Joe was rushing around, helping out wherever he could, full of excitement because his father was coming home. Finally all the adults were occupied inside the house and the young people were walking around in the yard, playing with Joe's dog, Samantha. The day was unusually warm and the sun was shining.

They were throwing sticks and Samantha was bringing them back when suddenly the dog stopped, perked up her ears, and gave a short bark. Then she raced off toward the road.

"My father is coming," Joe said. "She has picked up the scent!" He ran after Samantha, and the girls followed.

As they reached the main road, Mandie could hear wheels and hooves. In a moment the vehicle came into sight.

"It's Mr. Ginn bringing my father home from the depot," Joe said, looking up the road as the buggy approached.

The young people ran forward.

"Your grandmother is not with him, Faith!" Mandie excitedly told her friend.

A big smile crossed Faith's face as the buggy turned into the lane. "I'm so glad," she whispered.

Dr. Woodard waved to them as Mr. Ginn drove on to the house. The young people ran after the buggy, and by the time Dr. Woodard was stepping down, they were crowding around him with questions.

But the doctor spoke first to Faith. "The doctors in New York believe there is a possibility of helping your grandmother, and much as she disliked having to stay up there without you, Faith, she said to give you her love and tell you to wait for her a little longer," he said, taking his bag from the buggy.

"Oh, Dr. Woodard, I'm so thankful, to you and everybody," Faith said, so excited she could barely speak.

"That's good news, because we aren't finished working on her house yet," Joe said, taking the bag from his father.

"And it also means we'll have another party," Esther reminded him, clapping her hands.

"Oh, everything has turned out so happy!" Mandie said.

As everyone went into the house, Mandie thought about how things had worked out. All they had to do now was wait for Mrs. Chapman to return, and then they would celebrate again. As Mandie went in the back door, she glanced back at the bright blue sky.

"You've helped everybody else, dear God, now please help Mrs. Chapman. Thank you," she said softly.

And she had a sudden feeling that Mrs.

Chapman would return looking much better. Mandie looked up at the sky again and smiled.

One mystery has been solved—and a new one has begun! Mandie is convinced that the snowman outside her bedroom window can speak. Is she right? Find out in *The Talking Snowman.*

Picture Puzzle and Mandie's Missing Words

Mandie enjoys solving mysteries more than anything. She especially loves puzzles. Here are two for you: one to make and one to solve!

Picture Puzzle

When Mandie doesn't have a puzzle to solve, she makes one up. You can too!

Materials you will need:
a piece of poster board or other thin cardboard
(a shirt box lid or the back of a stationery pad,
for example) at least 5 by 7 inches
a picture the same size as or slightly smaller than
the board: a photograph, a magazine cutout,
or a drawing you made yourself (make sure to
get permission to use the picture you choose)

glue
waxed paper
pen or pencil
scissors

1. Ask an adult to help you spread a thin layer of glue on the back of your picture and glue it to the cardboard. Press down, making sure the glue doesn't bubble. Wipe off any extra glue.

2. Cover your picture with waxed paper. Place something heavy on top—a dictionary, for example—so that your picture doesn't curl. Allow it to dry for at least four hours.

3. Once your picture is dry, trim any extra cardboard from the edges. On the back of the cardboard, outline your puzzle pieces—draw lines that connect with one another. Your puzzle should have at least six pieces—the more oddly shaped, the better!

4. Cut your picture up, using the lines as your cutting guide.

5. Now you have a puzzle! Mix up the pieces and see if your family can put them back together!

Mandie's Missing Words

Mandie wrote a few sentences about the mystery she just solved. But somehow a word was erased in each sentence! Can you figure out the missing words without peeking back at the story? Good luck!

1. Faith's grandmother's last name is _____.

2. Mandie wonders whether Faith is telling the _____.

3. Joe's dog is named _____.

4. Mrs. Woodard and Mrs. Shaw make two _____ for Faith.

5. Irene has a crush on _____.

6. The missing teapot had pink _____ on it.

7. Miss Abigail's housekeeper is Miss _____.

8. When Dr. Woodard comes home, there is a _____ in his honor.

1. Chapman 2. truth 3. Samantha 4. dresses 5. Tommy Lester 6. rosebuds 7. Dicey 8. party

The Talking Snowman

Winter has arrived in Charley Gap! There's so much snow that Mandie and Joe make a huge snowman in Mandie's front yard. One night, after her family is asleep, Mandie hears someone talking outside her bedroom window. But no one is there except the snowman. And he can't talk . . . or can he? The answer is a surprise to everyone—including Mandie!—in this spirited mystery with a heartwarming solution.

Coming in March 2000!

About the Author

LOIS GLADYS LEPPARD has written many novels for young people about Mandie Shaw. She often uses the stories of her mother's childhood in western North Carolina as an inspiration in her writing. Lois Gladys Leppard lives in South Carolina.